WHALE IS STUCK

BY KAREN HAYLES & CHARLES FUGE

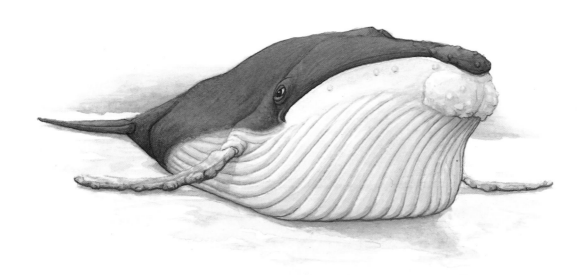

SIMON & SCHUSTER BOOKS FOR YOUNG READERS
Published by Simon & Schuster
New York ● London ● Toronto ● Sydney ● Tokyo ● Singapore

It was midsummer in the Arctic, and the sun shone all day and all night. The sheet of ice that had covered the sea during the winter was finally beginning to melt and break into small islands.

Whale loved the open sea. He swam down into the deep, dark blue water, where he turned and, thrusting his tail as hard as he could, aimed for the bright surface above.

Fish watched Whale splash
in and out of the water.
    "Look at me!" Whale cried
as he gave a huge leap up.

Fish quickly swam aside in case
Whale landed on top of him.
But this time there was no splash.

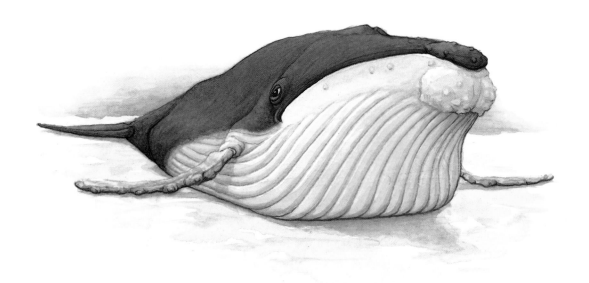

Whale had landed–SLAP–right in the middle
of an ice floe!

Poor Whale was stuck fast on the ice.

"What am I going to do now?" he spluttered.

Just then Walrus heaved himself onto the floe.
He'd been digging for clams on the seabed
when he saw Whale's enormous shadow appear
above him.

Before Walrus had a chance to ask Whale what
he was doing there, the Dolphins and Porpoises
had swum along to see what was happening.
The Dolphins were chattering so loudly that a
flock of nosy Sea Birds swooped in as well.

But down below the ice floe, Fish was becoming very curious. He could only see dim shapes through the thick ice. Why hadn't Whale come back down to see him?

Up above, Walrus had taken charge:
   "Dolphins!" he bellowed. "Try and tip the floe from underneath, and I will lever Whale off the ice with my magnificent tusks."

On the count of three, the Dolphins tipped up the ice floe and Walrus strained as hard as he could . . . but Whale was so heavy he didn't move an inch.

"We could try to lift you off," squawked
Puffin hopefully.
    And all at once the Birds flew up and perched
on top of Whale.

"Ouch! Stop!" shrieked Whale as the Birds tried
to grip his slippery skin with their sharp claws.
   "It looks as if I will be stuck forever,"
sighed Whale.

By now the crowd had grown even larger.
Some Seals had arrived and some inquisitive
Polar Bears.

Walrus puffed himself up to make another announcement.

"You Seals, come and help push while I lever Whale with my magnificent tusks and the Dolphins tip the ice floe. We'll soon have Whale back in the water!"

So the Seals pushed, Walrus strained and the
Dolphins tipped, but still Whale remained stuck
in the middle of the ice floe.

"Oh dear, oh dear," Walrus muttered into his
large, bristling mustache.

Poor Whale began to sob quietly to himself.

Suddenly, a long, spiraled spike appeared out of the sea. It was followed by the cheerful face of Narwhal.

"If Whale jumped onto the ice floe," he said, "then he should be able to jump off again."

"I think he just needs a little jab from underneath," Narwhal said thoughtfully.

Before Whale could protest, Narwhal had disappeared underwater and was heading for the dark shadow above.

His pointed tusk slid easily into the ice until–
THUMP!
It wasn't quite long enough to go right through.
Narwhal got a nasty bump on the nose.

Deep below the surface, Fish peered upward
and noticed that now the shadows were
becoming clearer.

Meanwhile, Walrus had another plan.

"If the Polar Bears leap onto the edge of the ice floe and the Dolphins tip the other side, I will lever Whale with my magnificent tusks while the Seals push."

So the Polar Bears leapt, the Dolphins tipped,
Walrus strained and the Seals pushed.

The ice floe reached an alarming angle, and then
fell back with a mighty . . .

. . . SPLASH!

A huge wave came over them and everyone was
swept clean off the ice . . . except Whale!

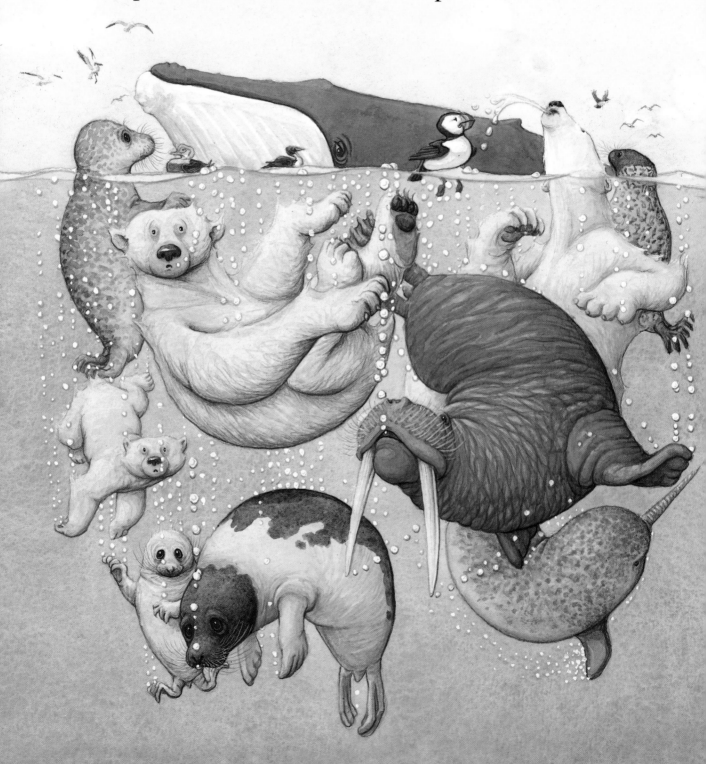

As the day went on, the sun got hotter and brighter. The animals continued to push and shove poor Whale until finally they gave up and lay hot and panting in the heat on the cool ice.

Beneath them, deep in the water, Fish peered upward. At last he could see everything clearly as the heat of the sun began to melt the ice floe. Fish knew that the ice must be very thin.

Above the surface, everyone was too tired to notice the tiny cracks that were appearing all around them. They were so tired that they didn't even notice the creaking noises the ice floe was making. Or the snapping noises as the tiny cracks got bigger.

Suddenly, there was a terrific **CRUNCH!**

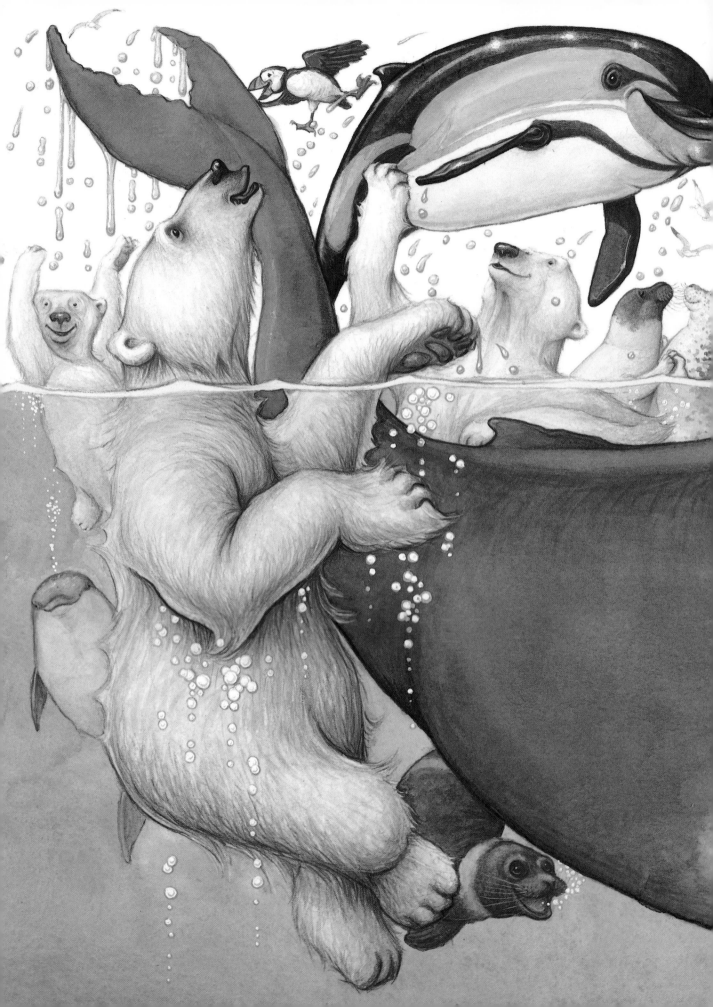

All the animals were plunged into the sea—
including Whale! When they all reached
the surface again, they realized what
had happened.

Whale was so pleased that he *almost* leapt out of the water, but then he remembered what had happened earlier that morning.

Whale also remembered that Fish was still waiting for him deep below. And with a slap of his tail, he went to join him.

SIMON & SCHUSTER BOOKS FOR YOUNG READERS
Simon & Schuster Building, Rockefeller Center
1230 Avenue of the Americas, New York, New York 10020
Text and illustrations copyright © 1992 by Karen Hayles and Charles Fuge.
a division of BBC Enterprises Limited. First U.S. edition 1993
SIMON & SCHUSTER BOOKS FOR YOUNG READERS is a trademark of Simon & Schuster.
Manufactured in China   10 9 8 7 6 5 4 3 2 1

Library of Congress Cataloging-in-Publication Data
Hayles, Karen. Whale is stuck / By Karen Hayles & Charles Fuge. p.   cm.
Summary: While leaping about in the open sea one day, Whale lands
on an ice floe, where all the Arctic animals attempt to get him back
into the sea where he belongs. [1. Whales—Arctic regions—Fiction.
2. Zoology—Arctic regions—Fiction.] I. Fuge, Charles. II. Title.
PZ7.F9513Wh   1993[E]—dc20 92-34078 CIP
ISBN: 0-671-86587-0

3